GREAT ILLUSTRATED CLASSICS

THE WIZARD OF OZ

L. Frank Baum

adapted by
Deidre S. Laiken

Illustrations by
Pablo Marcos Studio

BARONET BOOKS, New York, New York

GREAT ILLUSTRATED CLASSICS

edited by
Malvina G. Vogel

CONTENTS

They Follow the Yellow Brick Road.

About the Author

Lyman Frank Baum was born on May 15, 1856, in Chittenango, New York. He began his writing career as a teen-age reporter for the *New York World*. Within two years, he was the publisher of a small town newspaper in Pennsylvania.

As a young man, Baum also acted in road companies and wrote plays. One of his musical comedies was produced in New York. He returned to journalism in 1880. Lyman Baum married and had four sons. He settled in Chicago where he founded a trade journal, which helped him to support his family while he continued writing fiction.

The Wizard of Oz, which was first published in 1900, became so popular among its readers that Baum wrote thirteen sequels to the original story. In addition, he wrote books for girls under the pen name of Edith Van Dyne. L. Frank Baum died in 1919.

Characters You Will Meet

Dorothy   *the girl who is whisked by the cyclone to the land of Oz*

Toto   *her dog*

Aunt Em and Uncle Henry   *they hid in the cellar and never left Kansas*

Characters in the Land of Oz

The Wonderful Wizard of Oz

Dorothy's three friends
The Scarecrow
The Tinman
The Cowardly Lion

The four Witches
The Wicked Witch of the East
The Good Witch of the North
The Wicked Witch of the West
The Good Witch of the South

The Munchkins
The Queen of the Field Mice and All the Field
Mice
The Guardian of the Gate to the Emerald
City
The Winkies
The Leader of the Wolves and the Pack of
Wolves
The King Crow and the Wild Crows
The Swarm of Bees
The Monkey King and the Band of Winged
Monkeys
The Bending Trees
The China People in the Dainty China Coun-
try
The Hammer-Heads
The Quadlings

The Tiny House on the Prairie

Chapter 1

The Cyclone

Dorothy lived with her Aunt Em and Uncle Henry on a small farm in Kansas.

Their tiny house stood alone on a large, flat prairie. Dorothy had only one friend, her dog Toto. He was a small black dog who loved to jump and play.

One day while Dorothy and Toto were playing, they heard the awful sound of a storm. The wind roared and the dust blew smoky circles in the air. Dorothy was frightened.

Uncle Henry stopped working and shouted, "There's a cyclone coming, run for the cellar!"

A cyclone is a terrible storm. Even little Toto wanted to run away. He jumped from Dorothy's arms, ran into the house, and hid under the bed. Dorothy followed him into the house. Then a strange thing happened. The house turned around and around. Then it rose through the air! Toto ran out from under the bed and barked loudly.

It was very dark and the house swayed back and forth. Dorothy held Toto in her arms and listened to the wind. She was frightened. Aunt Em and Uncle Henry were safe in the cellar. She was all alone. Hours passed. The house tossed and turned in the storm. Finally Dorothy closed her eyes and fell asleep.

A Cyclone Is a Terrible Storm.

A Magical Land

Chapter 2

The Munchkins

After a long time, Dorothy woke up. Everything was very quiet. Bright sunshine came through the windows. Toto pressed his cold nose against Dorothy's face. "Where am I?" asked Dorothy. "What happened to Uncle Henry and Aunt Em?"

She ran to the door and looked out at a magical land. All around her were beautiful green trees and colorful flowers. Tiny purple birds sang as they flew from tree to tree. Dorothy had never seen such a lovely place.

Suddenly she heard a small voice say, "Welcome to the Land of the Munchkins."

Dorothy turned around and there were three men and one woman standing in a circle. They were all the same size as Dorothy, but they looked like grown-ups. They wore hats that rose to a small point about a foot above their heads. Tiny bells tinkled when they moved. The men wore strange blue suits and had long white beards. The woman wore a long gown covered with stars. She made a bow, and in a sweet voice said, "How can we thank you for killing the Wicked Witch of the East? You have set us free!"

Dorothy was shocked.

"There must be some mistake," she said. "I have not killed anyone."

The tiny woman pointed to the house.

"Look, your house landed on the Witch. Those are her feet sticking out from under a block of wood."

The Munchkins

"Oh dear!" cried Dorothy. "I'm so sorry."

"There is nothing you can do," said the woman. "She was a very wicked Witch, and she made the Munchkins slaves for many years. Now thanks to you, we are free!"

"Are you a Munchkin?" asked Dorothy.

"No," answered the woman. "I am the Good Witch of the North."

Dorothy had never heard of a good witch. But the kind woman explained that Dorothy was now in the Land of Oz. In the Land of Oz there were four witches. The witches who lived in the North and South were good witches, and the people loved them. But the witches who lived in the East and West were wicked.

"Now you have killed the Wicked Witch of the East," explained the gentle woman. "There is only one Wicked Witch still alive."

Now Dorothy understood. She was happy to have helped the Munchkins, but she wanted

The Good Witch of the North

to return to Kansas and see her Uncle Henry and Aunt Em.

The Good Witch and the Munchkins had never even heard of Kansas. Dorothy was a long, long way from home. She began to cry. She felt very lonely in this strange land.

When the Good Witch saw that Dorothy was crying, she took off her cap and balanced the point on the end of her nose. She counted to three. The cap changed into a slate. On the slate were the words, "Let Dorothy go to the Emerald City."

Dorothy dried her tears.

"You must go to the Emerald City. Maybe the Wizard of Oz can help you," said the Good Witch.

"Who is the Wizard of Oz?" asked Dorothy.

"He is a great Wizard," answered the Good Witch.

"He is more powerful than all of us put together. He lives in the Emerald City. Only he can help you return to Kansas."

"One—Two—Three."

"How can I get to the Emerald City?" asked Dorothy.

"You must walk," answered the Good Witch. "You will see a Yellow Brick Road. Follow that road and you will find the Wizard of Oz."

Then the Good Witch kissed Dorothy on the forehead. It was a magical kiss, and it left a round, shining mark. It would protect Dorothy on her long trip. The Munchkins gave Dorothy the silver slippers that the Wicked Witch of the East had worn. They had a special magic, but no one knew what it was.

Dorothy put on the silver slippers, waved good-bye to her new friends, and she and Toto began their journey to the Emerald City.

The Magical Kiss

The Scarecrow

Chapter 3

The Scarecrow

Dorothy and Toto followed the Yellow Brick Road for many miles. After a while, they stopped beside a big cornfield and sat down to rest. Not too far away, Dorothy could see a Scarecrow. It was placed high on a pole so it would scare the birds away from the ripe corn. The Scarecrow's head was a small sack stuffed with straw. Someone had painted its face with eyes, a nose and a mouth. It was dressed in a blue suit and wore old boots and a pointed blue hat.

While Dorothy was looking at the Scarecrow, she was surprised to see one of the eyes slowly wink at her. Then the figure nodded its head in her direction. Dorothy walked up to the Scarecrow.

"Good day," said the Scarecrow.

"Did you speak?" asked Dorothy.

"Certainly," answered the Scarecrow. "How do you do?"

"I'm pretty well, thank you," replied Dorothy. "How are you?"

"I'm not feeling well," said the Scarecrow. "This pole is stuck up my back, and I can't get down."

Dorothy reached up and lifted the figure off the pole. Since the Scarecrow was made of straw, he was very light.

"Thank you very much," said the Scarecrow. "I feel like a new man."

All this seemed very strange to Dorothy. She had never seen a stuffed man who could walk and talk.

Dorothy Lifts Him Off the Pole.

"Who are you and where are you going?" asked the Scarecrow.

"My name is Dorothy," she said, "and I am going to the Emerald City to ask the Great Oz to send me back to Kansas."

But the Scarecrow had never heard of the Great Oz or the Emerald City. Sadly he explained to Dorothy that since his head was stuffed with straw he had no brains. Dorothy felt very sorry for the unhappy Scarecrow.

"Do you think," he asked, "that if I go to the Emerald City with you, the Great Oz will give me some brains?"

"I cannot tell," she answered, "but you may come with me if you like. If Oz will not give you any brains, you will be no worse off than you are now."

The Scarecrow nodded his head in agreement and joined Dorothy and Toto on their journey to the Emerald City.

Setting Off for the Emerald City

"Shall We Go There?"

Chapter 4

The Tinman

After a few hours, the road began to get rough. Walking grew difficult, and the Scarecrow fell many times. But since he was made of straw, he never got hurt.

Soon the daylight faded away and the sky grew very dark. Dorothy could not see at all, but the Scarecrow said he could see in the dark just as well as in the light. Dorothy asked him to stop when he saw a house, for she was becoming very tired.

After a little while, the Scarecrow stopped:

"I see a cottage built of logs and branches. Shall we go there?"

"Oh yes!" answered Dorothy. "I am really very tired."

When they reached the cottage, Dorothy fell fast asleep with Toto beside her. The Scarecrow, who never needed to sleep, stood in a corner and waited for morning.

As the sun came up, Dorothy was wakened by an awful groan. The sound seemed to come from somewhere in the forest. Dorothy saw something shining not far from where she stood. When she walked deeper into the forest, she saw a remarkable thing. Standing beside a large tree was a man made completely of tin. He held an axe in his hand. Dorothy looked at him in amazement.

"Did you groan?" she asked.

"Yes," answered the Tinman.

"I've been groaning for a long time, but no one has ever come to help me."

A Man Made Completely of Tin

"What can I do for you?" asked Dorothy.

"Get an oil can and oil my joints," answered the Tinman. "They are so rusty I cannot move."

Dorothy ran back to the cottage and found an oil can. The Tinman told her where to put the oil. In just a few minutes the Tinman was able to move.

"How can I ever thank you?" he said. "I might have stood in the forest for years if you hadn't saved me. How did you happen to be here?"

Dorothy explained that she, Toto and the Scarecrow were all on their way to the Emerald City to see the Great Oz. When she told him this, the Tinman began to think.

"Do you suppose Oz could give me a heart?" he asked. "The Wicked Witch of the East cast an evil spell on me as I was out here chopping wood. She turned me into tin and took away my heart."

Oiling the Rusty Joints

Dorothy thought for a moment.

"Why, I think so," she answered. "It would be as easy as giving the Scarecrow brains."

So the Tinman picked up his axe and his oil can and joined his new friends on their journey to Oz.

The Tinman Joins His New Friends.

Toto Barks at the Lion.

Chapter 5

The Cowardly Lion

As Dorothy and her friends continued on their way through the forest, they heard a terrible roar. The next moment, a great Lion ran onto the road. Dorothy and her two friends were very frightened, but little Toto ran ahead and barked at the huge beast.

When the Lion saw the little dog, he opened up his mouth as if to bite him. Dorothy became so angry at this that she rushed forward and slapped the Lion on the nose.

"Don't you dare bite Toto!" she shouted.

"You ought to be ashamed of yourself, a big Lion like you, trying to bite a little dog!"

"I didn't bite him," said the Lion, as he rubbed his nose with his big paw.

"No, but you tried to," Dorothy answered. "You are nothing but a coward!"

The Lion hung his head in shame. He confessed to Dorothy and her friends that although he was supposed to be King of the Beasts, he really was a coward. Large tears fell from his eyes as he told the travelers his sad story. The poor Lion was afraid of almost everything and everybody.

The Scarecrow stopped for a moment and scratched his straw head. Then he said:

"I am going to the Emerald City to asks the Great Oz to give me brains. Maybe Oz could give you courage."

The Lion wiped away his tears.

"If I only had courage, then I could truly be King of the Beasts."

"If Only I Had Courage."

So Dorothy, the Scarecrow and the Tinman invited the Lion to join them on their journey to the Emerald City. The Lion agreed, and the friends continued to follow the Yellow Brick Road towards the home of the Great Oz.

They Follow the Yellow Brick Road.

The Field of Scarlet Poppies

There Is No Time to Rest.

So the Tinman and the Scarecrow made a chair with their hands and carried Dorothy slowly through the field.

After a while, they came to a bend in the river. There, lying fast asleep in the flowers, was the Lion. The smell from the poppies had been so strong that the huge beast had given up and fallen asleep.

The Scarecrow and the Tinman felt very sad. Since they could not carry the Lion because he was so heavy, they had no choice but to leave him there to sleep.

Carrying Dorothy Through the Field

A Large Yellow Wildcat

Chapter 7

The Queen of the Field Mice

The Scarecrow and the Tinman sat beside a river and waited for Dorothy to wake up.

"We can't be far from the Yellow Brick Road now," said the Scarecrow. "But which way do you suppose it is?"

The Tinman was about to answer, when he heard a low growl. He turned his head and saw a large yellow wildcat come running towards him. Its mouth was open, showing two rows of ugly, sharp teeth. Its red eyes glowed like balls of fire. It was chasing a tiny grey field mouse. Although he had no heart, the

Tinman knew it was wrong for the wildcat to try to kill such a tiny creature.

So the Tinman raised his axe, and as the wildcat ran by, he gave it a quick blow and cut the beast's head off.

"Oh, thank you, thank you ever so much for saving my life," said the field mouse in a squeaky voice.

"You are quite welcome," answered the Tinman. "Even though I have no heart, I am careful to help those who need a friend, even if it happens to be only a mouse."

The tiny mouse looked shocked.

"Why, I am the Queen—the Queen of all the Field Mice. And since you have saved my life, I owe you a good deed in return."

But the Tinman could not think of anything this tiny mouse could do to help him.

Just then the Scarecrow got an idea.

"I know something you could do to help us," he shouted. "Our friend, the Lion, is fast

The Queen of the Field Mice

asleep in the poppy field. Do you think you could help us move him?"

The Tinman could not understand how a tiny mouse could move a great Lion. But the Queen of the Field Mice informed him that she was queen of thousands of mice. She gave a signal, and in a few minutes they were surrounded by field mice. They came from all directions. There were big mice, and little mice, and middle-sized mice. Each one brought a piece of string in its mouth.

The Tinman and the Scarecrow worked very quickly, and in no time at all, they made a truck out of tree branches. They slowly tied one end of each piece of string around the neck of each mouse and fastened the other end to the truck. When all the mice had been harnessed to the truck, they were able to pull it quite easily.

The Tinman and the Scarecrow sat on the wooden truck while the tiny mice pulled

Each Mouse Brings a Piece of String.

them into the poppy field.

They soon found the Lion. They finally managed to get him on the truck, but they had to work very hard, for the Lion was very heavy. Then with the help of the Scarecrow and the Tinman, the mice were able to pull the truck out of the poppy field.

By this time, Dorothy and Toto were awake, and they were very happy to see their friend the Lion being pulled away from the deadly flowers.

The Queen of the Field Mice bowed and in a squeaky voice said:

"Good-bye, and if you ever need us again, come out into the field and call, and we shall hear you and help you any way we can—good-bye."

Hard Work!

The Gates of the Emerald City

Chapter 8

The Emerald City

The next morning as soon as the sun was up, Dorothy and her friends started on their way. Soon they saw a beautiful green glow in the sky.

"That must be the Emerald City," said Dorothy.

As they walked, the green glow became brighter and brighter. It seemed that at last they were at the end of their long journey.

Finally, they reached the end of the Yellow Brick Road. Before them stood a huge gate covered with emeralds. The jewels glittered in the sun.

Next to the gate was a bell. Dorothy rang the bell, and the big gate swung open very slowly. Inside was a large room covered with shining emeralds. A little man stood inside the room. He was dressed all in green. At his side was a large green box. He asked Dorothy and her friends why they had come to the Emerald City.

"We came here to see the Wizard of Oz," said Dorothy.

The man was so surprised at this answer that he sat down to think.

"It has been many years since anyone has come to see the Great Wizard," he said. "I hope that your business is important, because if you have come here for a foolish reason, he might get angry and destroy all of you."

But the Scarecrow assured the man that they had come on very important business.

"Why Have You Come Here?"

Then the small man explained that he was the Guardian of the Gate, and only he could take them to see the Great Oz. But before they could enter the wonderful city, everyone had to put on green glasses. The Guardian of the Gate explained that the glasses would prevent them from being blinded by the brightness of the Emerald City. He carefully unlocked the box and fitted everyone, even little Toto, with a pair of green glasses. Finally, they were all ready to enter the gates of the Emerald City.

Green Glasses for Everyone

Green Candies! Green Cookies!

Chapter 9

The Great Oz

Even though their eyes were protected by the green glasses, Dorothy and her friends were dazzled by the wonderful city. The streets were lined with beautiful houses which were all made of green marble and covered with sparkling emeralds.

There were many people—men, women and children, all dressed in green clothing. Several shops were open and Dorothy saw that everything in them was green. There were green candies, green cookies, and even glasses of green lemonade. Everyone seemed happy and comfortable in the Emerald City.

The Guardian of the Gate led them through the streets until they came to a big building, exactly in the middle of the city. This was the Palace of Oz. In front of the door stood a soldier. He was dressed in a green uniform and had a long green beard.

"Here are the strangers," said the Guardian of the Gate, "and they demand to see the Great Oz."

The soldier asked everyone to follow him inside the palace. Then he asked them to wait while he brought their message to the Great Oz.

They had to wait a long time before the soldier returned. When he finally came back, Dorothy asked:

"Have you seen Oz?"

"Oh, no," answered the soldier. "I have never seen him. But I spoke to him as he sat

A Soldier

behind a screen. I gave him your message.
He said that he will talk to each one of you.
But he will only see one of you each day. So
you must stay here at the Palace for a few
days. I will show you to your rooms."

The next morning, a young woman dressed
all in green came to see Dorothy. She gave
Dorothy a lovely green dress and even tied
a green bow around Toto's neck. Then the
woman led Dorothy and Toto to the Throne
Room of the Palace to see the Great Oz himself.

After waiting for a few minutes, a bell
rang. Dorothy walked into the Throne Room.
The room was very big, and all the walls were
covered with glistening emeralds. In the middle of the room stood a huge throne. It was
shaped like a chair and sparkled with gems.
In the center of the chair was an enormous
Head. There was no body, or arms or legs to
support the Head. It stood alone.

A Green Bow for Toto

Dorothy looked at the enormous Head with wonder and fear. The eyes in the Head turned slowly and the mouth moved. Then a voice said:

"I am Oz the Great and terrible. Who are you and why are you here?"

Dorothy was frightened, but somehow she had the courage to answer.

"I am Dorothy, and I have come to ask you to help me return to my home in Kansas."

The eyes looked at her for a few minutes, then a voice said:

"Where did you get those silver shoes, and what is that mark on your forehead?"

Dorothy explained that the shoes had belonged to the Wicked Witch of the East, and that the mark on her forehead was the magical kiss of the Good Witch of the North.

The eyes looked at her carefully. They winked three times, and they turned up to the ceiling and down to the floor and rolled

The Enormous Head

around so they could see every part of the room. Then the Great Oz was ready to give his answer:

"If you want me to help you return to Kansas, you must first do something for me. You must kill the Wicked Witch of the West."

Dorothy began to cry.

"I have never killed anything willingly," she explained. "And even if I wanted to kill the Wicked Witch, I would not know how."

But the Great Oz only said:

"That is my answer. Until the Wicked Witch dies, you will not return to Kansas. Remember that the Wicked Witch is very evil and ought to be killed. Now go, and do not return until she is dead."

Sadly, Dorothy left the Throne Room and told her friends what had happened. The Scarecrow, the Tinman and the Lion felt very sad, because they could not help Dorothy.

The next morning, the soldier with the

"You Have to Do Something for Me!"

green beard led the Scarecrow into the Throne Room. There sitting on the sparkling throne, was a Beautiful Woman dressed in green silk and covered with jewels. Large green wings grew from her shoulders.

The Scarecrow bowed and the Beautiful Woman said:

"I am the Great Oz. Who are you and what do you want?"

The Scarecrow was very surprised. He had expected to see the Head Dorothy had told him about. But he answered the Great Oz and explained that what he wanted more than anything else was to have brains.

Oz was quiet for a few minutes. Then he said:

"I never grant favors without something in return. If you will kill the Wicked Witch of the West, I will give you the best brains in all the land. You will be the wisest man there is."

The Beautiful Woman

The Scarecrow was confused.

"But you asked Dorothy to kill the Wicked Witch of the West," he said.

"So I did," answered Oz. "I don't care who kills her, but until she is dead, I will not grant your wish."

The Scarecrow returned to his friends. He told them that the Great Oz had appeared in the form of a Beautiful Woman but had refused to give him any brains until the Wicked Witch was killed.

The next morning, the Tinman was called into the Throne Room. This time the Great Oz appeared as a Terrible Beast. The creature was as big as an elephant and had a head like a rhinoceros. It had five arms and five long legs. Thick woolly hair covered its huge body. The Tinman had never seen such a terrible creature.

"I am Oz the Great and Terrible," spoke the Beast. "Who are you and what do you want?"

The Terrible Beast

The Tinman explained that he wanted a heart, so that he could love.

Oz waited only a minute before he replied. He explained to the Tinman that he would receive a wonderful heart only if he helped Dorothy and the Scarecrow kill the Wicked Witch of the West.

The Tinman bowed his head and slowly left the Throne Room. When he returned to his friends, he sadly told them what Oz had said.

The next morning it was the Lion's turn to talk to the Great Oz.

When he entered the Throne Room, he expected to see the great Head, the Beautiful Woman, or the Hideous Beast. But the Lion saw none of these. Instead, to his surprise, he saw a great Ball of Fire. The Ball of Fire was so fierce and glowing that he could hardly look at it. As the Lion moved away from the heat of the fire, he heard a quiet voice say:

"I am Oz the Great and Terrible. Who are you and what do you want?"

A Fierce, Glowing Ball of Fire

The frightened Lion answered:

"I am a cowardly Lion, afraid of everything. I came to beg you to give me courage so that I can become King of the Beasts."

The Ball of Fire burned for a time, and then the voice said:

"Bring me proof that the Wicked Witch is dead, and then I will give you courage."

The Lion was angry at the Great Oz, but he was too frightened to say anything. So he ran from the room and joined his friends.

After the Lion told Dorothy what had happened, she looked at him sadly.

"What shall we do now?" she asked.

"There is only one thing we can do," answered the Lion, "and that is to go to the Land of the Winkies, where the Wicked Witch lives, and destroy her."

"But suppose we can't destroy her?" said Dorothy.

"Then I will never have courage," said the Lion.

The Lion Runs from Oz.

"And I will never have a heart," said the Tinman.

"And I will never have brains," said the Scarecrow.

"And I will never see Aunt Em and Uncle Henry," cried Dorothy.

The four friends thought for a long time.

"I suppose we must try it, but I am sure I do not want to kill anybody, even to see Aunt Em again," said Dorothy.

So Dorothy and her friends decided to begin their journey the very next morning.

Making Plans to Leave

Returning the Green Glasses

Chapter 10

The Search for the Wicked Witch

Dorothy and her friends were led to the gates of the Emerald City. The Guardian of the Gate removed their green glasses and put them back in the green box. He wished them good luck and reminded Dorothy that the Wicked Witch was very mean and would try to make them her slaves.

After they had said good-bye to the Guardian of the Gate, they began to walk towards the West. Soon the hot sun made Dorothy and the Lion very tired. They lay down on the cool grass and fell asleep, while the Tinman and the Scarecrow kept watch.

While Dorothy and the Lion were sleeping, the Wicked Witch of the West was watching them. She had only one eye, but it was as powerful as a telescope, and she could see everything. So, as she sat by the door of her castle, she happened to look around, and she saw Dorothy lying asleep with her friends beside her.

The Wicked Witch was angry to find them in her country. She blew on a silver whistle that hung around her neck.

In a few seconds, a pack of wolves came running to her. They had long legs and fierce eyes and sharp teeth.

"Go to those people," said the Witch, "and tear them to pieces."

"Aren't you going to make them your slaves?" asked the Leader of the Wolves.

"No," answered the Wicked Witch, "one is

The Wicked Witch Calls Her Wolves.

made of tin, one is made of straw, one is a little girl, and one is a Lion. None of them is fit to work, so you may tear them to pieces."

"Very well," said the wolf. And he dashed away at full speed with the rest of the pack.

But the Scarecrow and the Tinman were wide awake, and they heard the wolves coming.

The Tinman grabbed his axe, and as the Leader of the Wolves ran towards him, he swung his arm and chopped off the wolf's head. As soon as each wolf came close, he killed it with his sharp axe. Soon forty wolves lay dead in a great heap.

When the Wicked Witch saw what the Tinman had done, she became even angrier than before. So she blew her silver whistle twice.

In a few minutes, a great flock of wild crows came flying towards her.

The Wicked Witch said to the King Crow:

"Fly at once to the strangers and peck out their eyes and tear them to pieces."

A Green Bow for Toto

The wild crows flew towards Dorothy and her friends. When she saw them coming, Dorothy was afraid.

But the Scarecrow said, "This is my battle. Lie down beside me and you will be safe."

So everyone but the Scarecrow lay down on the ground. The Scarecrow stood up and stretched out his arms. When the crows saw him, they were frightened and did not dare to come any closer.

But the King Crow said:

"It is only a stuffed man. I will peck his eyes out."

The King Crow flew at the Scarecrow, who caught it by the head and twisted its neck until it was dead. As each crow flew at the Scarecrow, he twisted its neck. Soon there were forty crows lying dead beside him.

When the Wicked Witch saw all her crows lying in a heap, she went into a terrible rage and blew her silver whistle three times.

The Scarecrow Frightens the Crows.

This time a great swarm of bees came flying to her. The Wicked Witch told the bees to sting Dorothy and her friends to death.

But the Scarecrow saw the bees coming. He scattered his straw over Dorothy, Toto and the Lion. This way, the bees flew at the Tinman, and their stingers broke off against the tin. The Tinman was not hurt, but all the bees died. Their bodies lay scattered in the field.

The Wicked Witch was so angry when she saw her bees lying in little heaps that she stamped her foot and tore her hair and gnashed her teeth. Then she called a dozen of her slaves, who were the Winkies, and gave them sharp spears. She told them to find the strangers and destroy them.

The Winkies were not brave people, but they had to obey the Wicked Witch, so they marched away.

When the Lion saw them coming, he gave

The Wicked Witch Is Angry.

a great roar. The poor Winkies were so frightened that they ran away as fast as they could.

When the Wicked Witch saw what had happened, she made up her mind how to act.

She sent to the cupboard and took out her Golden Cap. This Cap had a special charm. Whoever owned it could call three times upon the Winged Monkeys. These creatures would obey any order they were given. But no one could command the Winged Monkeys more than three times. The Wicked Witch had used the charm of the Cap twice before, so this was her last wish.

She put the Golden Cap on her head and stood on her left foot. Then she recited a secret charm. Soon, the sky darkened and a low rumbling sound could be heard. In a few minutes, the Witch was surrounded by a crowd of monkeys with huge and powerful wings on their shoulders.

The Wicked Witch ordered the Winged

A Great Roar!

Monkeys to destroy the strangers except for the Lion. She wanted him brought to her so she could make him her slave.

"Your commands shall be obeyed," said the leader. Then the Winged Monkeys flew away.

When they found the Tinman, the Monkeys grabbed him and carried him through the air. When they were over some sharp pointed rocks, they dropped the poor Tinman. He fell a great distance to the rocks, where he lay so battered and dented that he couldn't move.

The rest of the Monkeys caught the Scarecrow, and with their long fingers pulled all of the straw out of his clothes and his head. They made his hat, boots and clothes into a small bundle and threw it into the top branches of a tall tree.

After they had done this, the Monkeys threw pieces of rope around the Lion and wound many coils around his body, head and legs. When they were sure he was unable to

The Monkeys Drop the Poor Tinman.

bite or scratch, they lifted him up and flew away with him to the Witch's castle. At the castle, he was placed in a small yard with a high iron fence, so that he could not escape.

But Dorothy was not harmed at all. She stood with Toto in her arms and watched what the Monkeys did to her friends. The Leader of the Winged Monkeys flew up to her. His long hairy arms stretched out, and his ugly face grinned terribly. But when he saw the mark of the Good Witch's kiss on her forehead, he stopped short and motioned the others not to touch her.

"We dare not harm this little girl," he said to them, "for she is protected by the Power of Good, and that is greater than the Power of Evil. All we can do is to carry her to the castle of the Wicked Witch and leave her there."

So, they carefully lifted Dorothy in their arms and carried her to the castle.

Behind a High Iron Fence

The Wicked Witch was surprised and worried when she saw the mark on Dorothy's forehead. She knew that she could not hurt the girl in any way. When she saw Dorothy's silver slippers she began to tremble in fear, for she knew what a powerful charm belonged to them.

But the Wicked Witch was also very clever. She knew that Dorothy did not know the true power of the silver slippers. So the Wicked Witch laughed to herself and thought, "I can still make her my slave, for she does not know how to use her power." Then she said to Dorothy:

"Come with me; and see that you mind everything I tell you, for if you do not, I will make an end of you as I did of the Tinman and the Scarecrow."

The Witch led Dorothy through the castle until they came to the kitchen. Here, the Witch made Dorothy clean the pots and pans,

The Wicked Witch Is Worried.

sweep the floor, and feed the fire with heavy logs.

While Dorothy was hard at work, the Witch would go into the courtyard and harness the Lion like a horse. She wanted the Lion to pull her cart and take her wherever she wished to go. But as she opened the gate the Lion gave a loud roar and bounded at her so fiercely that the Witch was afraid and ran out and shut the gate again.

"If I cannot harness you," said the Witch, "I can starve you. You shall have nothing to eat until you do as I wish."

So after that she took no food to the imprisoned Lion. Every day she came to the gate at noon and asked, "Are you ready to be harnessed like a horse?"

And the Lion would answer, "No. If you come in this yard, I will bite you."

The reason the Lion did not have to do as the Witch wished was that every night, while

The Lion Will Not Pull the Cart.

the Witch was asleep, Dorothy carried him
food from the cupboard. After he ate, Dorothy
would sit beside him, and they would talk of
their troubles and try to plan some way to
escape. But they could not find a way to get
out of the castle, for it was always guarded
by the yellow Winkies, who were the slaves
of the Wicked Witch and too afraid of her not
to do as she ordered.

Dorothy worked very hard during the day,
and her life became very sad. She knew it
would be difficult to return to Kansas. Some-
times she held little Toto in her arms and
cried bitterly.

Now the Wicked Witch had a great longing
to own Dorothy's silver shoes. She knew the
power of these shoes would make her more
evil and feared than she already was. She
watched Dorothy carefully to see if she ever
took off her shoes, thinking she might steal
them. But Dorothy only removed them when

They Talk of Their Troubles.

she took her bath at night. The Witch was too afraid of the dark to dare enter Dorothy's room at night to take the shoes, and her fear of water was even greater than her fear of the dark, so she never came near when Dorothy took her bath. The old Witch never touched water and never let water touch her in any way.

But the Wicked Witch was very clever, and she finally thought of a trick so that she could get Dorothy's silver shoes. She placed an iron bar in the middle of the kitchen floor. Then she used her magic to make the bar invisible. In this way, she knew Dorothy would trip over the bar and loose her shoes.

But when Dorothy tripped over the invisible bar, she only lost one shoe. The Witch quickly snatched it and put it on her own foot. When Dorothy saw what had happened, she grew very angry and said, "Give me back my shoe!"

Dorothy Loses One Shoe!

"I will not," laughed the Witch. "Now it is my shoe, not yours. And someday I shall get the other one from you too."

This made Dorothy so angry that she picked up the bucket of water she had been using to wash the floor and threw it over the Witch.

Instantly the Witch gave a loud scream and then, as Dorothy looked in wonder, the Witch began to shrink and melt away.

"See what you have done!" she screamed. "In a minute I shall melt away."

"I'm very sorry," said Dorothy, who was truly frightened to see the Witch melting away like brown sugar.

In a few minutes the Witch turned into a brown, melted, shapeless mass and began to spread over the kitchen floor. All that was left of the Witch was the silver shoe. Dorothy picked it up, cleaned it, and put it back on her own foot.

The Witch Begins to Melt!

Then, being free at last, Dorothy ran out to the courtyard to tell the Lion that the Wicked Witch of the West had come to an end, and that they were no longer prisoners in a strange land.

Dorothy Comes to Free the Lion.

A Holiday!

Chapter 11

The Rescue

The Lion was very happy to hear that the Wicked Witch had been melted away, and Dorothy unlocked the gate of his prison and set him free. Next, Dorothy gathered all the Winkies together and told them that they were no longer slaves.

The Winkies were very happy, for they had been made to work hard for many years. They made the day of their freedom a holiday and spent the time feasting and dancing.

"If only our friends the Scarecrow and the

Tinman were with us," said the Lion, "I would be totally happy."

"Don't you think there is some way we could rescue them?" said Dorothy.

"We can try," answered the Lion.

So they called the Winkies and asked them to help rescue their friends. The Winkies said that they would be delighted to do something for Dorothy since she had set them all free. So a group of Winkies traveled that day and part of the next until they came to the rocky plain where the Tinman lay, all battered and bent. His axe was next to him, but the blade was rusted and the handle broken off.

The Winkies lifted him and carried him back to the castle. When they reached the castle Dorothy asked the Winkies if any of their people were tinsmiths. She found that there were several Winkies who were skilled tinsmiths. In a little while they came to the castle with baskets of tools. They looked the

The Winkies Carry the Tinman.

Tinman over carefully and told Dorothy that they thought they could mend him so he would be as good as ever.

The Winkies worked for three days and three nights. They hammered, twisted and pounded at the legs, body and head of the Tinman. At last he was straightened out into his old form, and his joints worked as well as ever.

When at last he walked into Dorothy's room and thanked her for rescuing him, he was so happy that he cried tears of joy. Dorothy and the Lion were so happy to see their friend that they danced and celebrated all day.

"If only we had the Scarecrow with us again," said the Tinman, "I would be truly happy."

"We must try to find him," said Dorothy.

So she called the Winkies to help her, and they walked all that day and part of the next

Tears of Joy

until they came to the tall tree where the
Winged Monkeys had tossed the Scarecrow's
clothes. The Tinman quickly chopped the tree
down, and Dorothy and the Winkies carried
the Scarecrow's clothes back to the castle. As
soon as they entered the castle, the Winkies
began stuffing the clothes with nice, clean
straw. Soon the Scarecrow stood before
them—as good as ever! He thanked them
over and over again for saving him.

Now that they were reunited, Dorothy and
her friends spent a few happy days at the
castle, where they found everything they
needed to make themselves comfortable.

But after a few days, they all decided that
it was time to return to Oz and ask for the
things that they had been promised.

So they sadly said good-bye to the Winkies
and packed food and blankets for the journey
back to the Emerald City.

The Winkies Stuff the Scarecrow.

"We Have Lost Our Way."

Chapter 12

The Winged Monkeys

The next morning, Dorothy and her friends began their journey to the Emerald City. They walked a long way and still could not see a sign of the Emerald City. And since they had been carried to the castle by the Winged Monkeys, they were not at all sure in which direction they should walk.

Days passed, and they still saw nothing but the fields and forests. The Scarecrow began to complain.

"We have surely lost our way," he said, "and unless we find it again in time to reach the Emerald City, I shall never get my brains."

"Nor I my heart," said the Tinman.

"And I do not have the courage to keep tramping forever, without getting anywhere at all," said the Lion.

Dorothy sat down on the grass to think.

"Suppose we call the field mice," she suggested. "They could probably tell us the way to the Emerald City."

"To be sure they could!" cried the Scarecrow. "Why didn't we think of that before?"

Dorothy blew the whistle that the Queen of the Field Mice had given her. In a few minutes they heard the pattering of tiny feet, and many of the small grey mice came running up to her. The Queen herself came up to Dorothy.

"What can I do for my friends?" she squeaked.

"We have lost our way," answered Dorothy.

Dorothy Blows the Whistle.

"Can you tell us where the Emerald City is?"

Certainly," answered the Queen, "but it is a great way off, for you have had it at your backs all the time." Then she noticed Dorothy's Golden Cap and suggested that Dorothy use the Golden Cap to call the Winged Monkeys, who would carry everyone to the Emerald City.

So Dorothy recited the magic words that were written inside the Golden Cap. In a few minutes she heard the chattering and flapping of wings, as the band of Winged Monkeys flew up to her. The King bowed low before Dorothy and asked:

"What is your command?"

Dorothy explained that they had lost their way, and wished to be taken to the Emerald City. No sooner had she spoken than the Monkeys picked up Dorothy, Toto, the Tinman, the Scarecrow and the Lion, and carried them in their long hairy arms all the way to

The Winged Monkeys Fly to Dorothy.

the Emerald City.

The journey took a very short time. When they reached the gates of the Emerald City, the Monkeys set them all down carefully. Then the King bowed to Dorothy and flew swiftly away, followed by all his band.

"That was a good ride," said Dorothy.

"Yes, and a quick way out of our troubles," answered the Lion. "It certainly was lucky that you remembered to bring that Golden Cap!"

The Monkeys Set Them Down.

The Guardian of the Gate Greets Them.

Chapter 13

Oz the Terrible

Dorothy and her friends walked up to the gate of the Emerald City and rang the bell. After they rang many times, the Guardian of the Gate answered the bell.

"What! Are you back already?" he asked in surprise.

"We certainly are!" answered the Scarecrow.

"But I thought you had gone to find the Wicked Witch of the West," said the Guardian of the Gate.

"We did find her," said the Scarecrow, "and Dorothy melted her away."

"Melted! Well, that is good news," said the Guardian of the Gate.

He led them into his little room and gave them all green eyeglasses just as he had done before. Then they passed through the big gates into the Emerald City. When the Guardian of the Gate told the people that Dorothy had melted the Wicked Witch of the West, they all gathered around the travelers and followed them in a great crowd to the Palace of Oz.

Once they reached the Palace gates the soldier with the green beard greeted them and carried the news of their arrival to the Great Oz. Dorothy thought that once he heard the news, the Great Oz would send for her at once, but he did not. Dorothy and her friends waited for many days, but still heard nothing from the Great Oz.

A Great Crowd

The waiting was tiresome, and at last they grew angry at Oz for treating them so badly. So the Scarecrow sent a message to Oz which said that if he did not see them at once, they would call the Winged Monkeys to help them and find out whether he kept his promises or not. When the Wizard was given this message, he was so frightened that he sent word for them to come to the Throne Room at four minutes after nine o'clock the next morning. Oz had met the Winged Monkeys once, and he knew their power. He was very afraid of meeting them again.

The four travelers found it difficult to sleep that night. Each thought of the gift Oz had promised to give them. Dorothy fell asleep dreaming of Kansas and her Aunt Em.

At nine o'clock the next morning, the soldier with the green beard came to escort them to the Throne Room.

Dorothy, the Tinman, the Scarecrow and

The Little Man Hangs His Head.

the Lion all expected to see the Wizard in the shape he had taken before. They were all surprised when they saw that the room was empty.

Soon they heard a Voice that seemed to come from somewhere near the top of the great dome, and it said solemnly:

"I am Oz the Great and Terrible. Why do you seek me?"

They looked again in every part of the room and still saw no one. Dorothy asked, "Where are you?"

"I am everywhere," answered the Voice, "but if you wish to talk with me, walk near the Throne."

So they walked toward the Throne and Dorothy said:

"We have come to claim our promises."

"What promises?" asked Oz.

Dorothy repeated the Wizard's promise to send her back to Kansas, and to give the Tin

"We Have Come to Claim Our Promises."

man a heart, the Scarecrow brains, and the Lion courage.

"Is the Wicked Witch really destroyed?" asked the Voice.

"Yes," answered Dorothy, "I melted her with a bucket of water."

"Dear me," said the Voice, "how sudden! Well, come to me tomorrow, for I must have time to think it over."

This made the Scarecrow and the Tinman very angry, and they began to shout at the Great Oz, and they demanded that he keep his promises to them. The Lion thought that he might as well frighten the Wizard, so he gave a large, loud roar. This was so frightening that Toto jumped away from him and tipped over a screen that stood in the corner of the room. As it fell with a crash they looked and saw a very strange thing. For, standing in just the spot the screen had hidden, was a little old man with a bald head and a wrin-

The Lion's Roar Frightens Toto.

kled face. The man seemed just as surprised as Dorothy and her friends. The Tinman raised his axe and rushed towards the little man and shouted, "Who are you?"

"I am Oz the Great and Terrible," said the little man in a trembling voice, "but please don't hit me—please don't—and I will do anything you want."

Dorothy and her friends were surprised and upset.

"We thought Oz was a Great Head, a Ball of Fire, a Terrible Beast, or a Beautiful Woman," said the Scarecrow.

"No, you are wrong," said the little man. "I have been making believe."

"Making believe," cried the Tinman. "Are you not a great Wizard?"

The little man hung his head in shame and confessed that he was only a common man who was able to perform some clever magic tricks. He asked Dorothy and her friends to sit down while he told them his strange story.

The Little Man Hangs His Head.

The Wizard Begins His Story.

Chapter 14

The Magic of the Great Oz

Dorothy and her friends sat down in some comfortable chairs while the Wizard told them this story:

"I was born in Omaha. When I grew up I became a ventriloquist and learned how to throw my voice, so it seemed to come from many places at once. I was well trained by a great master. I can imitate any kind of bird or beast." Then he mewed like a kitten, and Toto pricked up his ears and looked everywhere to see where the sound was coming from.

"After a while I got tired of doing that and decided to become a balloonist. A balloonist is someone who goes up in a balloon on circus day and attracts a crowd of people who pay to see the performance. Well, one day I went up in a balloon, and the ropes got so twisted that I couldn't come down again. The balloon went way up above the clouds, and a current of air struck it and carried it many, many miles away. For a day and a night I traveled through the air, and on the morning of the second day I awoke and found the balloon floating over a strange and beautiful country.

"My balloon came down gradually, and I was not hurt. But I found myself among strange people. They had seen me come out of the clouds and thought I was a great and powerful Wizard. Of course I let them think this, because they were afraid of me and promised to do anything I asked them to.

Floating Over a Beautiful Land

"So I ordered them to build this City and to construct this Palace. They did it all willingly. Then, I thought that since everything in this country was so green and beautiful, I would call it the Emerald City. To make the name fit even better, I put green eyeglasses on all the people. This way everything they saw was green."

"But isn't everything here green?" asked Dorothy.

"No more than in any other city," answered Oz. "But when you wear green glasses, of course everything looks green to you. The Emerald City was built many years ago when I was a young man. I am very old now. But the people here have worn green glasses for so long that most of them think this really is an Emerald City. I have been good to the people here, and they have been good to me. But since this palace was built I have shut myself up, and I have refused to see anyone.

"Isn't Everything Here Green?"

"One of the things I have feared most is the evil power of the Witches. Since I have no magical powers at all, I knew that their powers could destroy me. I have lived in deadly fear of them for many years. I was very happy when I heard that your house fell on the Wicked Witch of the East, When you came to me, I was willing to promise anything if you would only do away with the Wicked Witch of the West. Now that you have melted her, I am ashamed to say that I cannot keep my promises."

"I think you are a very bad man," said Dorothy.

"Oh, no, I am really a very good man, but I will admit that I am a very bad Wizard," said Oz.

"Can't you give me some brains?" asked the Scarecrow.

"You don't need them. You learn something every day. Experience is the only thing

"I Am a Good Man, but a Bad Wizard."

that brings knowledge."

"That may be true," said the Scarecrow, "but I will be very unhappy unless you give me brains."

"Well," Oz said with a sigh, "I am not much of a magician, as I said, but if you come to me tomorrow morning I will stuff your head with brains."

"Oh, thank you—thank you," cried the Scarecrow.

"But how about my courage?" asked the Lion anxiously.

"You have plenty of courage. All you really need is some confidence in yourself. Every living thing is afraid when it faces danger. True courage is facing danger even when you are afraid, and you already have that kind of courage."

"Maybe I have," answered the Lion, "But I am scared just the same. I would like you to give me the sort of courage that makes me

"Oh, Thank You!"

forget to be afraid."

"Very well, I will give you that sort of courage tomorrow," said Oz.

"What about my heart?" asked the Tinman.

"I think you are lucky not to have a heart, for the heart is what makes most people unhappy," said Oz.

"That is your opinion," said the Tinman. "For my part, I will bear all the unhappiness without a word if you will give me the heart."

"Very well," answered Oz meekly. "Come to me tomorrow and you will have your heart. I have played Wizard long enough. I may as well continue for a little while longer."

Then Dorothy asked Oz how he would get her back to Kansas. The Wizard confessed that her request would take a little longer to fulfill. He asked them all to stay in the Palace for a few more days while he thought of a way to get Dorothy back to Kansas. In the

"What About My Heart?"

meantime, he asked them to keep his secret.

They all agreed to say nothing about what they had learned and went back to their rooms in high spirits, for they were all sure their wishes would be granted.

Their Wishes Will Be Granted.

The Wizard Sits by the Window.

Chapter 15

Oz Grants Three Wishes

The next morning, the Scarecrow went to see Oz and get his brains. He went to the Throne Room and knocked at the door.

"Come in," said Oz.

The Scarecrow went in and found the little man sitting by the window.

"I have come for my brains," said the Scarecrow.

"I have not forgotten," said Oz. "But I must take your head off in order to put your brains in their proper place."

"That's all right," said the Scarecrow. "You

are quite welcome to take my head off, as long as it will be a better one when you put it on again."

So the Wizard unfastened the Scarecrow's head and emptied out the straw. Then he went to the back room and mixed a cup of cereal with many pins and needles. He shook the mixture again and again. Then he filled the top of the Scarecrow's head with the mixture and stuffed the rest of the space with straw to hold it all in place.

When he fastened the Scarecrow's head back on his body again, Oz said, "From now on, you will be a great man, for you have brains."

The Scarecrow was pleased and proud, and he thanked the Wizard again and again.

When Dorothy saw the Scarecrow with all the needles and pins sticking out of his head, she was very surprised.

"How do you feel?" she asked him.

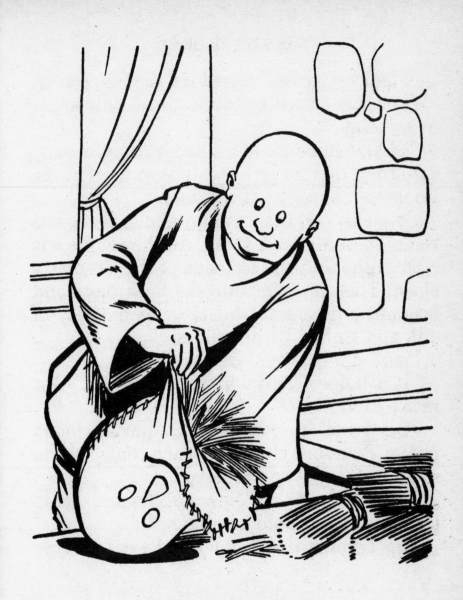

The Scarecrow's Brains

"I feel very wise," answered the Scarecrow. "When I get used to my brains I will know everything."

"Well, I must go to Oz and get my heart," said the Tinman. So he walked to the Throne Room and knocked at the door.

Oz welcomed the Tinman and said he was ready to give him a wonderful heart. He cut a small hole in the left side of the Tinman's chest. Then he went into the back room and brought out a pretty heart made entirely of silk and stuffed with sawdust.

"Isn't it a beauty?" Oz asked.

"It is indeed!" answered the Tinman. "But is it a kind heart?"

"Oh, very!" answered Oz. He put the heart in the Tinman's chest and then replaced the square of tin he had removed.

"There," he said. "Now you have a heart that any man would be proud of."

The Tinman thanked Oz and went back to

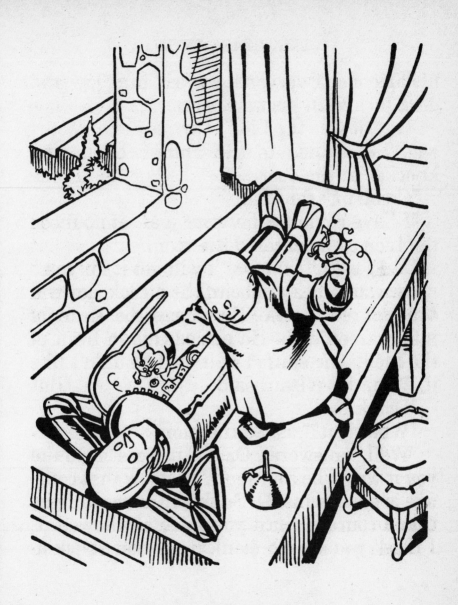

The Tinman's Heart

his friends. Everyone wished him joy and good luck with his new heart.

Next, it was the Lion's turn to get his courage. He walked to the Throne Room and knocked at the door.

"Come in," said Oz.

"I have come for my courage," announced the Lion as he entered the room.

"Very well," said Oz, "I will get it for you."

He went to a cupboard and took down a square green bottle. He poured the contents into a green dish. He placed this in front of the Lion, who sniffed at it as if he didn't like it. Then the Wizard said:

"Drink."

"What is it?" asked the Lion.

"Well," answered Oz, "if it were inside of you it would be courage. You know that courage is always inside. So this cannot really be called courage until you have swallowed it. I think you should drink it as soon as possi-

Oz Takes Down a Square Green Bottle.

ble."

The Lion did not hesitate and drank until the dish was empty.

"How do you feel now?" asked Oz.

"Full of courage," answered the Lion. Then he went back to tell his friends of his good fortune.

Oz smiled to think of his success in giving the Scarecrow and the Tinman and the Lion exactly what they thought they needed. It was easy to make them happy, because they imagined that he could do anything. But Oz knew that it would be much more difficult to take Dorothy back to Kansas, and he was very worried because he was not at all sure how it could be done.

The Lion Drinks.

Ready to Face an Army

Chapter 16

How the Balloon Was Launched

For three days, Dorothy did not hear from Oz. This made her very sad and worried. The Scarecrow was very happy with his new brain and told everyone about the wonderful thoughts he had. The Tinman could feel his heart rattling around in his chest when he walked. He told Dorothy that in only a few days he had discovered how to be tender and kind. The Lion declared that he wasn't afraid of anything on earth, and that he would gladly face an army of men or a dozen fierce beasts.

Each one had his wish granted except for Dorothy, who wanted more than ever to return to Kansas.

After four days, Oz sent for Dorothy. When she entered the Throne Room, he said pleasantly:

"Sit down, my dear. I think I have found a way to get you out of this country."

"And back to Kansas?" she asked.

"Well, I am not sure about Kansas, since I am not really sure where it is. But the first thing to do is to cross the desert, and then it should be easy to find your way home. And there is only one way to cross the desert. I have been thinking the matter over, and I believe I can make a balloon which will carry you over the desert.

"How do you make a balloon?" asked Dorothy.

"A balloon," said Oz, "is made of silk, which is coated with glue to keep the gas in it. There

"Sit Down, Dear."

is plenty of silk in this city but there is no gas to fill the balloon so that it will float."

"If it won't float," said Dorothy, "it cannot help us cross the desert."

"True," answered Oz. "But there is another way to make it float. We can fill it with hot air. Of course, hot air is not as good as gas, for if the air should get cold the balloon will come down in the desert, and we will be lost."

"We!" cried Dorothy. "Are you going with me?"

"Yes, of course," said Oz. "I am tired of being such a fake. I don't want my people to discover that I am not a Wizard at all. I'd much rather go back to Kansas with you and be in the circus again."

So Dorothy and Oz cut the strips of silk and sewed them neatly together. When they finished this, Oz sent one of his soldiers to search for a large clothes basket. He tied the basket to the bottom of the balloon with many ropes.

Sewing the Silk Strips

He explained to Dorothy that they would ride in the basket.

When the balloon was finally finished, Oz sent word to his people that he was going to make a visit to a great brother Wizard who lived in the clouds. The news spread through the city, and everyone came to see the wonderful sight.

Oz ordered the balloon carried out in front of the Palace, and the people looked at it with curiosity. The Tinman chopped a big pile of wood and then made a fire of it. Oz held the bottom of the balloon over the fire so that the hot air rising from it would be caught inside. Soon the balloon swelled out and rose into the air, until finally the basket just touched the ground.

Then Oz got into the basket and said to all the people:

"I am going away for awhile. During the time that I am gone the Scarecrow will rule

The Curious Balloon

over you. I command you to obey him as you would obey me."

By this time, the balloon was tugging at the rope that held it to the ground. Since the air inside was hot, it was much lighter in weight than the air outside the balloon. The balloon was beginning to rise into the sky.

"Hurry up, Dorothy!" cried the Wizard, "or the balloon will fly away."

"I can't find Toto anywhere," answered Dorothy. Toto had run into the crowd to bark at a kitten. When Dorothy finally found him, she picked him up and ran toward the balloon.

She was only a few steps away, and Oz was holding out his hands to help her into the basket, when the ropes went—crack! The balloon rose into the air without her.

"Come back!" shouted Dorothy.

But it was too late. Oz was already riding in the basket, rising farther and farther into

"Hurry Up, Dorothy!"

the sky.

And that was the last any of them saw of Oz. No one ever knew if he reached Omaha safely, but everyone remembered him lovingly, and they were very sad to see him go.

Oz Drifts into the Sky.

Dorothy Is Very Unhappy.

Chapter 17

The Journey to the South

At first Dorothy was very unhappy about missing her chance to return to Kansas. She cried a lot that first day. But when she thought it all over, she was glad she did not go up in a balloon, although she also felt sorry about losing Oz.

The Scarecrow was now the ruler of the Emerald City. Although he was not a Wizard, the people were all proud of him. They bragged that there was not another city in all the world ruled by a stuffed man.

The morning after the balloon went up, the

four travelers met in the Throne Room to talk matters over. The Scarecrow sat in the big Throne, and the others sat in soft chairs beside him.

"We are all very lucky," he said, "for this Palace and the Emerald City belong to us, and we can do just as we please. When I remember that a short time ago I was up on a pole in a farmer's cornfield, and that now I am the ruler of this beautiful City, I am quite happy with what has happened to me."

The Tinman and the Lion expressed their satisfaction with the rewards Oz had granted them, and they too said they were content. Only Dorothy was still unhappy. She told her friends that although she loved them all very much, she still wanted to return to her home in Kansas.

The Scarecrow decided to think. He thought so hard that the pins and needles began to stick out of his brains.

The Scarecrow Sits in the Big Throne.

"Why not call the Winged Monkeys and ask them to carry you over the desert?"

"I never thought of that!" said Dorothy. "I'll go get the Golden Cap."

When she brought the Cap into the Throne Room, she spoke the magic words, and soon the band of Winged Monkeys flew in the open window and stood beside her.

"This is the second time you have called us," said the Monkey King. "What is your wish?"

"I want you to fly with me to Kansas," said Dorothy.

"That cannot be done," said the Monkey King. "We belong to this country alone, and we cannot leave it. There has never been a Winged Monkey in Kansas, and I suppose there never will be. We just do not belong there. We will be glad to serve you in any way we can, but we cannot cross the desert. Good-bye."

The Winged Monkeys Fly In.

The Monkey King bowed and then flew away through the window, followed by all his band.

Dorothy was almost ready to cry, she was so disappointed.

"I have wasted the charm of the Golden Cap for nothing," she said, "for the Winged Monkeys cannot help me."

The Scarecrow began thinking again, and his head bulged so much that Dorothy was afraid it would burst.

"Let's call in the soldier with the green beard," he said, "and ask his advice."

When the soldier entered the Throne Room, the Scarecrow asked him if he knew how Dorothy might cross the desert. The soldier explained that he knew of no one except Oz who had ever crossed the desert.

"Is there no one who can help me?" asked Dorothy.

The soldier thought a minute. Then he

The Scarecrow's Head Bulges.

said:

"Perhaps Glinda can help you. She is the Good Witch of the South. She is the most powerful of all the Witches and rules over the Quadlings. Besides, her castle stands on the edge of the desert, so she may know a way to cross it."

"How can I get to her castle?" asked Dorothy.

"The road is straight to the South," he answered, "but it is said to be very dangerous for travelers."

When the soldier left, the Scarecrow said:

"It seems that in spite of the dangers, the best thing Dorothy can do is to travel to the Land of the South and ask Glinda for help. This will be the only way Dorothy will ever get back to Kansas."

The Lion, the Tinman and the Scarecrow thought for only a second, and then all said they would go with Dorothy. The journey

"How Can I Get to Glinda's Castle?"

would be long and dangerous, and they could not let their friend go all by herself.

Dorothy thanked them all, and they decided to return to their rooms and get ready for their long journey, which would begin at sunrise the next morning.

Dorothy Thanks Her Friends.

Sleeping on the Grass

Chapter 18

The Fighting Trees

The next morning, Dorothy and her friends said good-bye to the Guardian of the Gate and left the Emerald City.

The first day's journey was through the green fields and bright flowers that stretched around the Emerald City on every side. That night they slept on the grass and looked up at the velvet sky filled with bright stars.

In the morning they traveled until they came to a forest. The forest was very thick, and there seemed to be no way to go around it. So they looked for the place where it would be the easiest to get into the forest.

The Scarecrow discovered a big tree with wide-spreading branches that would allow everyone to pass underneath. But just as he came under the first branches they bent down and twined around him. The next minute, he was lifted from the ground and thrown through the air. This did not hurt the Scarecrow, but it surprised him, and he looked dizzy when Dorothy picked him up.

"Here is another space between the trees," called the Lion.

"Let me try it first," said the Scarecrow, "for it doesn't hurt me to be thrown around." He walked up to another tree. But immediately its branches grabbed him and tossed him back again.

"This is very strange," said Dorothy. "What shall we do?"

"The trees seem to have made up their

Grabbed by the Branches!

minds to fight us and stop our journey," said the Lion.

"Let me give this a try," said the Tinman. He put his axe on his shoulder and walked up to the first tree that had thrown the Scarecrow in the air. When a branch bent down to grab him, the Tinman chopped it in half. The tree began shaking in pain, and the Tinman walked safely under it.

"Come on!" he shouted to the others. "Hurry up!"

They all ran forward and passed under the tree without being hurt. The other trees did not try to stop them. So they decided that only the first row of trees could bend down their branches, and that these were the police force of the forest, who tried to keep strangers away.

The travelers walked to the edge of the forest. Then, to their surprise, they saw a high wall which seemed to be made of china. It

The Tinman Chops the Branch in Half.

was smooth like the surface of a dish, and much higher than their heads.

"What will we do now?" said Dorothy.

"I will make a ladder so we can climb over the wall," said the Tinman.

"I Will Make a Ladder."

The Scarecrow Watches the Tinman.

Chapter 19

The Dainty China Country

While the Tinman was making a ladder from wood which he found in the forest, Dorothy lay down and slept. She was very tired from the long walk. The Lion also curled up to sleep and Toto lay beside him.

The Scarecrow watched the Tinman while he worked and said to him:

"I cannot figure out why this wall is here or what it is made of."

"Rest your brains and do not worry about the wall," answered the Tinman. "When we have climbed over it we will know what is on the other side."

After a while the ladder was finished. It looked clumsy, but the Tinman was sure it was strong and would serve the purpose of getting them over the china wall. The Scarecrow woke Dorothy, Toto and the Lion. He told them that the ladder was ready. The Scarecrow climbed up the ladder first, but he was so awkward that Dorothy had to follow close behind to keep him from falling off. When he got his head over the top of the wall and could see, he said, "Oh, my!"

"Go on," shouted Dorothy.

So the Scarecrow climbed further up and sat down on the top of the wall, and Dorothy looked over and cried, "Oh, my!" just like the Scarecrow had done.

Then Toto came up and immediately began to bark, but Dorothy told him to be quiet.

The Lion climbed the ladder next, and then

Up the Ladder

the Tinman. Both of them said, "Oh, my!" as soon as they looked over the wall. When they were all sitting in a row on the top of the wall they looked down and saw a very strange sight.

Before them was a great stretch of land. The floor of the land was as smooth and shining and white as the bottom of a big plate. Scattered around were many houses made entirely of china and painted in bright colors. These houses were very small. The biggest one reached only as high as Dorothy's waist. There were also tiny barns painted red with china fences around them. There were cows, sheep, horses and pigs, all made of china.

But strangest of all were the people who lived in this unusual country. There were milkmaids and shepherdesses, who wore red and yellow blouses and skirts with golden spots. There were princesses with beautiful dresses of silver, gold and purple. The shep

Houses Made Entirely of China

herds were dressed in short pants with pink, yellow and blue stripes on them. Their shoes had golden buckles. There were princes with jeweled crowns and ermine robes. There were also clowns in ruffled gowns with round red spots on their cheeks and tall, pointed caps. But the strangest thing of all was that all these people were made of china. Even their clothes were made of china. And they were so small that the tallest one was no higher than Dorothy's knee.

At first, none of the little people even looked at the travelers. One little purple china dog with an extra-large head came to the wall and barked at them.

"How can we get down the other side of this wall?" asked Dorothy.

The ladder was so heavy they couldn't pull it up, so the Scarecrow fell off the wall. Then the others jumped down on him so the hard floor would not hurt their feet. They were

Tiny People Made of China

very careful not to land on his head and get the pins stuck in their feet. When they were all safely down, they picked up the Scarecrow and patted his straw back into shape.

"We must cross this strange place in order to get to the other side," said Dorothy, "for we really must continue going South."

They began walking through the country of the china people, and the first thing they came to was a china milkmaid milking a china cow. As they came near, the cow gave a kick and over went the stool, the pail and even the milkmaid herself. Everything fell on the china ground with a great clatter.

Dorothy was shocked to see that the cow had broken its leg off, and that the pail was lying in several small pieces. Even the milkmaid had a nick in her left elbow.

"See what you have done!" cried the milkmaid angrily. "My cow has broken her leg, and I must take her to the mender's shop and

Over Goes the Milkmaid!

have it glued on again. What do you mean coming here and frightening my cow?"

"I am really very sorry," said Dorothy. "Please forgive us."

But the milkmaid was too angry to answer. She picked up the leg and led the cow away. The poor animal limped on three legs.

Dorothy felt very bad about what had happened.

"We must be very careful here," said the kind-hearted Tinman, "or we may hurt these little people so they will never get over it."

A little further on Dorothy met a beautifully dressed Princess. The Princess stopped short when she saw the strangers, and she started to run away.

Dorothy wanted to see more of the Princess, so she ran after her, but the china girl cried out:

"Don't chase me! Don't chase me!"

She had such a frightened voice that Dorothy stopped and asked, "Why not?"

The Princess Starts to Run Away.

"Because," answered the Princess, "if I run, I may fall down and break myself."

"But you could be mended, couldn't you?" asked Dorothy.

"Oh, yes; but one is never as pretty after being mended, you know," answered the Princess.

"I suppose not," said Dorothy.

"Now there is Mr. Joker, one of our clowns," continued the china woman, "who is always trying to stand on his head. He has broken himself so many times that he is mended in a hundred places and doesn't look at all pretty. Here he comes now, so you can see for yourself."

Indeed, a jolly little clown came walking by, and Dorothy could see that in spite of his pretty clothes of red, yellow and green, he was completely covered with cracks. It was clear that he had been mended in many places.

The Clown Is Covered with Cracks.

Dorothy felt sad for the poor little clown. Then she turned to the beautiful Princess and said:

"You are so lovely, I am sure that I could love you dearly. I am going back to Kansas. Won't you let me carry you back in my basket, so when I get back home I can stand you on Aunt Em's mantelshelf?"

"That would make me very unhappy," answered the china Princess. "You see here in our own country we live happily and can talk and move around as we please. But whenever any of us are taken away our joints at once stiffen, and we can only stand straight and look pretty. Of course, that is all that is expected of us when we are on mantelshelves and cabinets and living room tables. Our lives are much more fun here in our own country."

"I understand," said Dorothy, "and I would not want to make you unhappy for anything in the world, so I will just say good-bye."

"Our Lives Are Fun Here."

"Good-bye," answered the Princess.

They walked carefully through the china country. Little animals and people scampered out of their way, afraid they would be broken.

Soon they reached the other side of the country and came to another china wall. It was not as high as the first one, and by standing on the Lion's back they all managed to scramble to the top. Then the lion gathered his legs under him and jumped the wall. Just as he did this he upset a china house with his tail and smashed it to pieces.

"That was too bad," said Dorothy, "but I think we were lucky that we did these people so little harm. They are all so delicate!"

"They certainly are," said the Scarecrow, "and I am thankful I am made of straw and cannot be hurt so easily. There are worse things in the world than being a Scarecrow."

Scrambling to the Top

"They are so afraid of outsiders," said the Tinman. "They must have been treated badly by those who did not understand them."

Dorothy nodded her head in agreement as she took her last look at the china wall.

Before them lay a gloomy forest.

Dorothy Nods in Agreement.

A Steep Hill

Chapter 20

The Country of the Quadlings

The four travelers passed through the forest safely. When they came to the edge of the forest they saw a steep hill covered from top to bottom with large pieces of rock.

"This will be a difficult climb," said the Scarecrow, "but we must get over this hill."

So he led the way and the others followed. They had just reached the first rock when they heard a voice cry out, "Keep back!"

Then from behind the rock stepped out the strangest man any of them had ever seen.

He was short and stout and had a big head

which was flat at the top and supported by a thick, wrinkled neck. He had no arms at all. The Scarecrow saw this and did not think that such a helpless creature could prevent them from climbing the hill. So he said, "I am sorry not to do as you ask, but we must pass over this hill whether you like it or not."

As fast as lightning, the man's head shot forward, and his neck stretched out until the flat part of his head hit the Scarecrow in the stomach and sent him falling over down the hill. Then the creature's head returned to the body, and he laughed and said, "It is not as easy as you think!"

A chorus of laughter came from the other rocks, and Dorothy saw hundreds of the armless Hammer-Heads on the hillside.

They realized that it was hopeless to attempt to fight these strange creatures.

"Let's call the Winged Monkeys," said the Tinman.

The Hammer-Head

So Dorothy put on the Golden Cap and said the magic words. In a few minutes the Monkeys stood before her. Dorothy ordered the King of the Monkeys to carry them over the hill and into the country of the Quadlings.

At once, the Monkeys picked them up and flew away with them. As they passed over the hill the Hammer-Heads yelled with anger and shot their heads high in the air, but they could not even come close to the Winged Monkeys.

After they had been set down in the country of the Quadlings, the King of the Monkeys said good-bye to Dorothy and quickly flew away.

The country of the Quadlings was rich and happy. The fields were full of wheat, and there were pretty rippling brooks and well-paved roads. The houses were all painted bright red. The Quadlings were short and fat and looked chubby and happy. They dressed

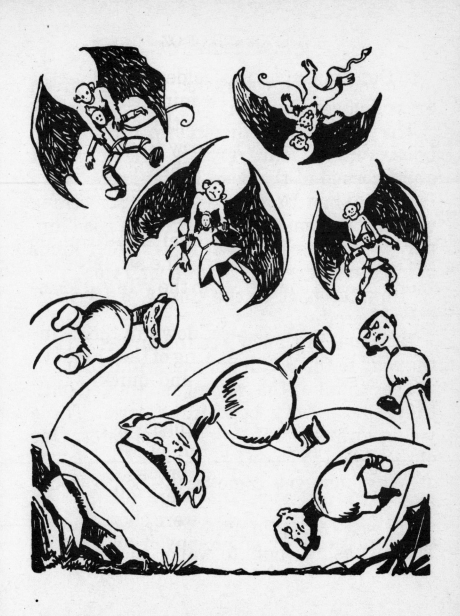

The Hammer-Heads Cannot Catch Them.

all in red, which contrasted with the green grass and yellow grain.

The Monkeys set them down near a farm house, and the four travelers walked up to it and knocked at the door. It was opened by a farmer. When Dorothy asked for something to eat, the woman gave them all a good dinner, with three kinds of cake and four kinds of biscuits and a bowl of milk for Toto.

"How far is it to the Castle of Glinda?" asked Dorothy.

"It is not far," answered the farmer. "Take the road to the South and you will find it."

They thanked the woman and walked until they saw a very beautiful Castle. Three young girls stood in front of the gates. One of them said to Dorothy:

"Why have you come to the South Country?"

"To see the Good Witch," she answered. The girl asked them to wait a moment and

The Quadlings

went inside the Castle to tell Glinda they had come.

The Girl Asks Them to Wait.

A Beautiful Witch

Chapter 21

Glinda Grants Dorothy's Wish

After a few moments, the girl came back to say that Dorothy and the others were to be admitted to the Castle at once.

Before they went to see Glinda, they were taken to a room where they washed and fixed themselves up.

When they were all quite presentable they followed the girl into a big room where the Witch Glinda sat upon a throne or rubies.

She was a beautiful Witch. Her hair was a rich red and fell in curls and waves over her shoulders. Her dress was pure white, but her eyes were blue, and they looked kindly upon Dorothy.

"What can I do for you, my child?" she asked.

Dorothy told the Witch her long story. She left out nothing. She talked for a long time.

"My greatest wish now," she added, "is to get back to Kansas, for Aunt Em must be very worried."

Glinda leaned forward and kissed Dorothy's face.

"Bless your dear heart," she said. "I am sure I can tell you how to return to Kansas. But if I do you must give me the Golden Cap."

"Of course!" said Dorothy. "It is of no use to me now, and when you have it you may command the Winged Monkeys three times."

Glinda smiled knowingly, and Dorothy handed her the Golden Cap. She turned to the Scarecrow and asked, "What will you do when Dorothy has gone back to Kansas?"

Glinda Kisses Dorothy.

"I will return to the Emerald City and be the ruler there," he answered.

Then Glinda asked the Tinman and the Lion where they would go after Dorothy had returned to her home. The Tinman thought for a moment and answered that he wished to return to the Land of the Winkies, and the Lion wanted to go back to his forest and be King of the Beasts.

Glinda knew that the journey back to these places would be long and difficult. So she explained that she would use the power of the Golden Cap to grant the Scarecrow, the Tinman and the Lion their wishes. The Winged Monkeys would carry them safely to their destinations.

The Scarecrow, the Tinman and the Lion thanked the Good Witch for her kindness. Then Dorothy said:

"You are certainly as good as you are beautiful! But you have not yet told me how to get back to Kansas."

They Thank the Good Witch.

"Your silver shoes will carry you over the desert," answered Glinda. "If you had only known their power you could have gone back to your Aunt Em the very first day you came to this country."

"But then I would not have gotten my wonderful brains!" cried the Scarecrow.

"And I would not have received my kind heart," said the Tinman. "I might have stood and rusted in the forest forever!"

"And I would have always been a coward," said the Lion, "and no beast in all the forest would have a good word to say about me."

"This is all true," said Dorothy, "and I am glad I could help my friends. But now that they have got their wishes and are happy, I think I would like to return to my home in Kansas."

"The silver shoes have wonderful powers. They will take you any place in the world in just three steps. All you have to do is knock

"Your Silver Shoes Will Carry You."

the heels together three times and command the shoes to carry you wherever you wish to go," explained Glinda.

"If that is so," said Dorothy, "I will ask them to carry me back to Kansas."

She kissed the Lion, the Tinman and the Scarecrow good-bye. They all cried and hugged her tightly.

Glinda stepped down from her throne and kissed Dorothy good-bye. Dorothy thanked her for her kindness.

Then Dorothy took Toto in her arms, said one last good-bye to her friends, and clapped the heels of her shoes together three times and said:

"Take me home to Kansas!"

In a few seconds she was whirling through the air so fast that all she could see or feel was the wind whistling past her ears.

Whirling Through the Air

Happy to Be Home Again

Chapter 22

Home Again

Aunt Em had just come out of the house to water the cabbages when she looked up and saw Dorothy running toward her.

"My darling child!" she cried, as she held Dorothy in her arms and covered her face with kisses. "Where in the world did you come from?"

"From the Land of Oz," said Dorothy. "And here is Toto too. And Aunt Em, I am so happy to be home again!"